B-10

For Chloe, Elena, and Marissa,
who keep inventing new ways to make me smile.
—K. H.

To Nonna Marisa
—V. F.

STERLING CHILDREN'S BOOKS
New York

An Imprint of Sterling Publishing Co., Inc.
1166 Avenue of the Americas
New York, NY 10036

ISBN 978-1-4549-2174-5

Distributed in Canada by Sterling Publishing Co., Inc.
c/o Canadian Manda Group, 664 Annette Street
Toronto, Ontario, M6S 2C8, Canada
Distributed in the United Kingdom by GMC Distribution Services
Castle Place, 166 High Street, Lewes, East Sussex, BN7 1XU, England
Distributed in Australia by NewSouth Books
45 Beach Street, Coogee, NSW 2034, Australia

For information about custom editions, special sales, and premium and corporate purchases,
please contact Sterling Special Sales at 800-805-5489 or specialsales@sterlingpublishing.com.

Manufactured in China

Lot #:
2 4 6 8 10 9 7 5 3 1
10/17

Design by Ryan Thomann
The artwork was created using pencil, ink, and digital media.

sterlingpublishing.com

MAGNOLIA MUDD and the SUPER JUMPTASTIC LAUNCHER Deluxe

by KATEY HOWES illustrated by VALERIO FABBRETTI

STERLING CHILDREN'S BOOKS
New York

EVERY FRIDAY,
my uncle Jamie Mudd comes over
to invent with me.
He is my absolute
favorite grown-up.
MUDD

Uncle Jamie never says boring stuff like "Sit still!" or "Don't touch that."

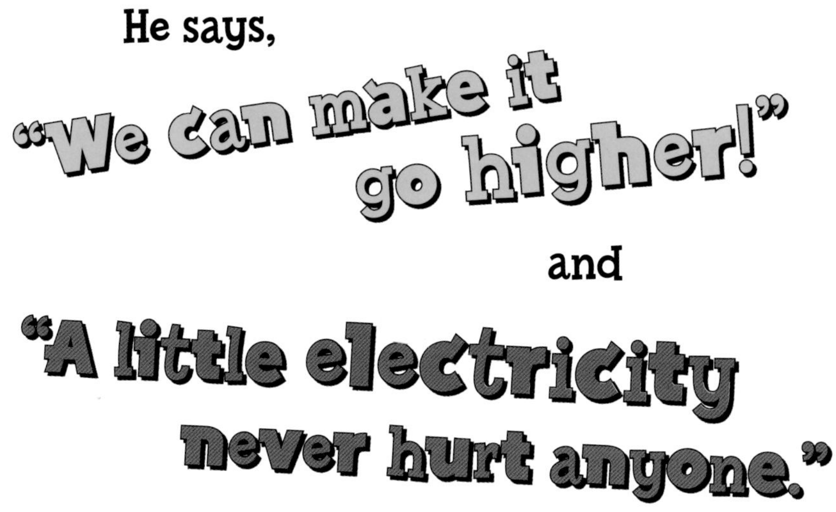

He says,

"We can make it go higher!"

and

"A little electricity never hurt anyone."

I do love electricity, but our greatest invention—
the SUPER **JUMPTASTIC ROCKET LAUNCHER** Deluxe—
runs on my favorite source of energy:

MUDD POWER!

Even the best inventions
need some tweaking.

I finally retrieved all the pieces, but I was going to need help putting them back together. When I called Uncle Jamie, he said the repairs would have to wait.

He said he was bringing Miss Emily over on Friday.
He said we had "something to talk about."

NOT FAIR! Fridays are my Uncle Jamie time. And Miss Emily ruins everything. I could never see why my uncle liked her.

See?

Nothing in common.

So this kind of took me by surprise.

"We're getting married!"

"We want you to be our flower girl!" Miss Emily said. "Just look at this dress!"

There was **no way** I was wearing that. Or tossing petals. Who has time for ribbons and bows when there are nuts and bolts to tighten?

I took evasive maneuvers.

“Maggie,” Uncle Jamie called. “Being a flower girl isn’t the only job in a wedding. We can think of something else.”

“Maybe something that takes Mudd Power?” I asked.

Uncle Jamie's eyes twinkled.

"Definitely."

Uncle Jamie dumped out dozens of wedding books and magazines.

“Find something that suits you,” he said.

"Wedding Style—
Gag!
1,001 Beautiful Bouquets—
Absolutely not.
Wedding Traditions
Around the World—
Hmmm.
This has potential."
MARRIED
90°
WEDDING
TRADITIONS
AROUND THE
WORLD

WEDDING TRADITIONS AROUND THE WORLD • 49

INDIAN BRIDES often decorate their feet and hands with Mehndi, or henna.

Henna tattoos looked cool.
But it would take way too
long to do them by hand.

I hooked our leaf blower to a jug of paint, added a hose and nozzle, whipped up some super-cool stencils, and took my creation for a test drive.

Back to the drawing board!

60 • WEDDING TRADITIONS AROUND THE WORLD

IN SWEDEN, guests bring stinky weeds to weddings to scare off trolls.

Weeds? How positively primitive! What I needed were bars, bait, and a motion detector.

My Mudd-mazing Troll Trap would be way more effective than weeds . . .

once I fixed a few glitches.

WEDDING TRADITIONS AROUND THE WORLD • 81

GERMAN wedding guests throw plates at the couple's door for good luck.

Everybody needs good luck, right? Especially when they've got nothing in common.

I dusted off my Fantastic Frisbee Flinger, added two extra flinging arms, and powered it up.

"Nuts, bolts, and sprockets!!"

I **knew** I should have used paper plates.

With no Mudd-powered plan, it looked like I was doomed to ruffles and roses.

Rather than scattering the petals, I wished I could **launch** them into the stratosphere. . . .

"When we jump on this part," I explained,
"air rushes through the hose over here. . . . "

"And my bouquet flies out over there!"
Miss Emily exclaimed. "I love it!"

Hmmmm. . . .
If she liked
that idea . . .

"We could make it even BIGGER!"
I suggested.
"So it can shoot more than flowers."

Miss Emily
grinned.

We grabbed goggles, tools, and glue. There was work to be done.

On the big day, we unveiled our new-and-improved DUAL-DIRECTIONAL **SUPER-JUMPTASTIC FLOWER LAUNCHER** Deluxe (with Confetti Blaster)!

Best of all, now that Aunt Emily was part of my family, we had way more Mudd Power for launching the bouquet.

MUDD

Maybe there's such a thing as **too much** Mudd Power.

UP
B-10